Published by Hachette Partworks Ltd
ISBN: 978-1-906965-22-8
Date of Printing: December 2009
Printed in Singapore by Tien Wah Press

ALICE
in
WONDERLAND

Disney

Ⓗ hachette

Once upon a time there lived a little girl called Alice. One day Alice was listening to her history lesson.

"Alice! You're not paying attention," her sister scolded.

"But it's dull!" Alice moaned. "The book needs pictures."

"Nonsense!" her sister said.

"In my world, every book would have pictures," Alice replied. "And everything would be nonsense!"

Later, Alice was resting in the soft grass. She thought about her special world and began to fall asleep.

Suddenly a white rabbit ran by.

"I'm late! I'm late! I'm late!" he cried. It was a talking rabbit! In a coat! With a pocket watch!

"Mr Rabbit, wait!" Alice called after him.

"I'm late for a very important date. No time to talk, I'm late, I'm late!" he answered. Then he disappeared down a rabbit hole.

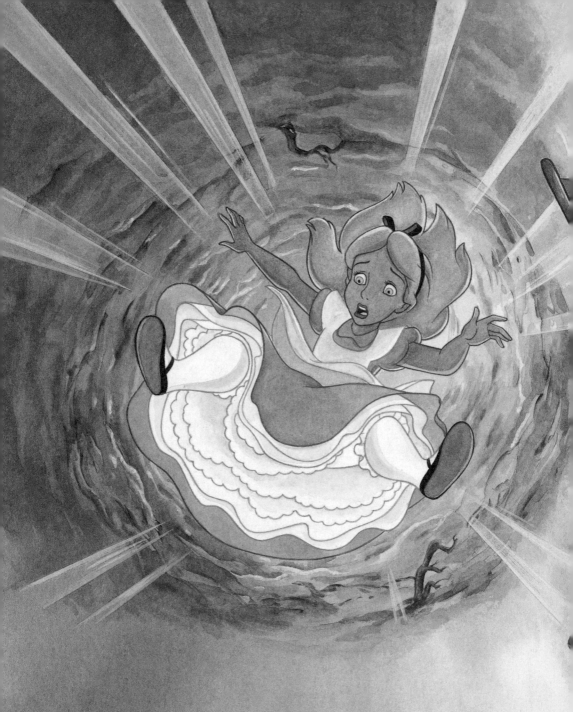

Alice was curious, so she followed the rabbit into the hole. It was dark. She crawled forward.

Then the ground disappeared! Alice fell. But she fell very slowly.

Strange objects passed by her: a lamp, a mirror, a rocking chair. And still she fell.

"Perhaps I'll fall right through the Earth and out the other side," Alice thought.

Finally, Alice reached the bottom. There she saw a little door.

"Pardon me," Alice said. "May I enter?"

"You're too big," the doorknob said. "Try the bottle."

Alice saw a little bottle marked "DRINK ME". So she did. Suddenly she shrank! Now Alice was small enough to fit through the door. But it was locked.

"You forgot the key!" the Doorknob said.

Alice saw the key on top of a table, but she was too small to reach it.

"Now try the box," the Doorknob said. Inside the box was a cookie saying "EAT ME". Alice ate. She grew into a giant!

"Oh, no!" Alice sobbed. She cried and cried. Her giant tears filled the room with water!

"The bottle!" the Doorknob cried.

Alice drank more and shrank again. This
time she became so small, she fell inside
the bottle! Suddenly she was swept through
the door on an ocean of tears.

Alice saw a strange dodo and other birds
floating along beside her.

"Mr Dodo! Help me! Please!" she cried.
But he didn't hear her.

Alice was soon washed ashore, where she saw the Dodo again. "Run with the others," the Dodo instructed, "or you'll never get dry."

But Alice ran after the White Rabbit instead.

Alice followed the rabbit into a forest, where she
met Tweedledee and Tweedledum.

"I'm looking for the White Rabbit," Alice told
them.

"Why?" asked Tweedledum.

"Well, I'm curious," Alice replied.

"Ah!" the twins replied. "The oysters were
curious, too!" Then they told Alice the story of the
curious oysters.

One day the Walrus and his friend the Carpenter were walking on the beach. The Carpenter saw something very interesting below the water.

"Walrus!" the Carpenter called. "You must see this!"

Under the water was a group of young oysters.

"Come with me," the Walrus said to the oysters. "We'll see many things: shoes, ships, sealing wax, cabbages and kings!"

The curious oysters followed the sneaky walrus.

The Walrus led them to a restaurant with only one thing on the menu – oysters! He ate all the curious oysters! He didn't even share with his friend.

"How sad!" Alice commented.

"Yes!" sobbed Tweedledum. "Now, there's a lesson to learn!"

As the twins cried, Alice quietly slipped away.

Alice wandered further into the forest. Soon she met a big blue caterpillar.

"Who are you?" the Caterpillar asked.

"I hardly know, sir," Alice answered. "I've changed my size so many times!"

The Caterpillar stood up and
began to spin round and round.
When he stopped, he had turned
into a beautiful butterfly!

"Here's a tip," he said. "One
side will make you larger,
the other side will make you
smaller."

"Other side of what?" Alice
asked.

"The mushroom, of course!"
he shouted as he flew away.

Alice was tired of
being three inches tall.
She broke off a piece of
mushroom from each side.
She ate one and... shoom!

She grew taller than the trees!
"Oh, dear!" Alice cried. "Will I ever get the
hang of this?"

She gently licked
the other piece. Alice
shrank back down to
normal size. "Now,
that's better," she said.

Alice continued her search for the White
Rabbit, but soon she was lost. Then she
heard a voice up in a tree.

"Diddledeedum… duddledaadidle…
caddledeedum," sang the voice.

Alice looked up. She didn't see anything.
Then a smiling face magically appeared.

"Why, you're a cat!" Alice said.

"A Cheshire cat," he replied as his body appeared from nowhere.

"I'm looking for the White Rabbit," Alice said. "Where should I go?"

"Where do you want to go?" the Cheshire Cat asked.

"Well, I don't know!" Alice answered.

"Then it doesn't matter!"

"If I were looking for a rabbit, I'd stand on my head!" the silly cat said.

"You could ask the March Hare; he's to the left. I'd ask the Mad Hatter; he's to the right."

"He really is mad, but most everyone here is! As you can see, even I'm not all there!"
Then the Cheshire Cat disappeared.

Alice walked to the Mad Hatter's house.

She heard voices singing. It was the Mad Hatter, the March Hare and the Dormouse. They were having a tea party. Alice sat down.

"You can't sit! It's rude!" the March Hare said.

"I'm sorry," Alice replied. "But I liked your singing."

"You did? Really?" the Mad Hatter asked. "Then you must join us."

"Yes, join our un-birthday party," the March Hare added.

"Un-birthday?" Alice asked.

"Yes," the Mad Hatter explained. "There are 365 days in a year. You only have one birthday and 364 un-birthdays!"

"I see," Alice said. "But I'm looking for the White Rabbit. The cat said…"

"CAT?" shouted the Dormouse, who had been sleeping in a teapot. He jumped out and ran around the table.

"You see what you did?" the Mad Hatter yelled at Alice.

"I'm sorry," Alice said. "But I really don't have time for this silliness."

"Time? I have no time! I'm late!" It was the White Rabbit!

"No wonder!" the Mad Hatter cried. "Your watch is two days late! I'll fix it."

The Mad Hatter fixed the watch with butter, cream, sugar and, of course, tea.

"Oh, my poor watch!" the rabbit cried, running off.

Alice grew tired of the
mad tea party. She left.
"What silly nonsense!"
she said. "I've had enough
nonsense. I'm going home."
    Alice walked further into
the forest. She came to a
sign marked "Tugley Wood"
and followed it.

TUGLEY
WOOD

Soon Alice was surrounded by all kinds of strange, nonsensical animals.

"Oh, no!" Alice cried. "I can't take any more. I wish I had never dreamed of a world where everything was nonsense!"

Then Alice heard a familiar song.

"Diddledeedum… duddledaadidle… caddledeedum…"

"Oh, Cheshire Cat, it's you!" Alice called. "I've had enough. I want to go home, but I've lost my way."

"That's because all ways here are the Queen's ways," he replied.

"Queen? What queen?" Alice asked.

"You haven't met her?" the cat asked. "Oh, you must! She'll be mad about you!"

Then a doorway opened in the tree.

Alice entered. Soon she heard three playing cards singing about painting roses red.

"Why are you doing that?" Alice asked the three playing cards.

"We planted white roses by mistake!" the two of Clubs replied. "The Queen of Hearts likes red. If she finds out, she'll chop off our heads!"

Alicc hurried to help them.

Suddenly the sound of drums and trumpets blared! "It's the Queen!" the cards cried. The Queen is coming!"

Alice and the cards got down on their knees.

"Announcing her Royal Majesty, the Queen of Hearts!" the White Rabbit proclaimed. "Oh, and the King, too," he added.

"Why, you're a little girl!" the Queen said, looking at Alice. "What are you doing here?"

"I want to go home," Alice answered. "But I've lost my way."

"Your way?" the Queen roared. "Every way is my way! Remember that!"

Then the Queen invited Alice to play a game of croquet. But what a game! Instead of a ball, the Queen used a hedgehog. And instead of a mallet, she used a flamingo!

The Queen finished
her shot. Then it was
Alice's turn. Alice
tried, but the flamingo
wouldn't play along!

"Do you want us both to lose our heads?"
Alice asked the silly flamingo.

Alice got angry. She grabbed
the bird and whacked the ball as
hard as she could! The shot was
better than the Queen's. The Queen
was furious!

"Off with
her head!" she
screamed.
"Uh, shouldn't
we have a trial
first, dear?" asked
the King.
"Oh, very well!"
the Queen replied
angrily.

Everybody gathered round the
Queen in her court.

"Hear ye! Hear ye!" the White Rabbit
cried. "Court is now in session!"

"But what have I done?" Alice
pleaded.

"Silence!" the Queen demanded.
"Oh, forget the trial! Let's just cut off
her head!"

Alice stuck her hands into
her pockets. She found a piece
of mushroom. She quickly ate it
and grew into a giant!

"Now, see here," Alice said to the
shocked queen. "You have no right to
treat me like this. You're no queen.
You're a nasty, bad-tempered old tyrant!"
    But the mushroom's effect was
wearing off. Alice shrank back down to
her regular size!

Oh, no! Alice was in trouble. She ran!

Soon Alice saw the small door she had used to enter this nonsense world.

Alice grabbed the Doorknob. "I must get out!" she cried.

"You are out," the Doorknob said. "See for yourself."

Alice looked through the keyhole. She saw herself sleeping under the tree.

"Wake up! Wake up!" she yelled. "Alice!"

"Alice! Alice!"
Alice woke up. She was back.
"Alice!" her sister said. "You were dreaming. What nonsense!"
"Yes, it was fun, but I've had enough nonsense to last me for quite some time! Shall we go home now?"